AUG 2 3 2

DIEGO'S INTERNATIONAL RESCUE LEAGUE ★ LEAGUE ★

adapted by Tina Gallo
based on the screenplay by Rosemary Contreras
illustrated by Art Mawhinney

Simon Spotlight/Nickelodeon
New York London Toronto Sydney

Based on the TV series *Go, Diego, Go!*™ as seen on Nick Jr.™

SIMON SPOTLIGHT
An imprint of Simon & Schuster Children's Publishing Division
1230 Avenue of the Americas, New York, New York 10020
© 2010 Viacom International Inc. All rights reserved.
NICKELODEON, NICK JR., *Go, Diego, Go!*, and all related titles, logos, and characters are trademarks of Viacom International Inc.
All rights reserved, including the right of reproduction in whole or in part in any form.
SIMON SPOTLIGHT and colophon are registered trademarks of Simon & Schuster, Inc.
For information about special discounts for bulk purchases, please contact Simon & Schuster Special Sales at 1-866-506-1949
or business@simonandschuster.com.
Manufactured in the United States of America 0710 LAK
First Edition
2 4 6 8 10 9 7 5 3 1
ISBN 978-1-4424-0793-0

¡Hola! I'm Diego, and I'm an Animal Rescuer. This is my *papi*. We are on our way to Rescue Island! Do you want to come, too, and be a part of my Rescue League team? *¡Excelente! ¡Al rescate!*

Rescue Island is a supersecret island with lots of different animal habitats. Rescuers come from all over the planet to see if they're ready to be World Animal Rescuers—just like my *papi*! I'm taking the World Animal Rescuer Test today with some other kids who will be part of my Rescue League team. Do you want to meet them? *¡Fantástico!*

Juma knows all about the deserts of Africa. Shanti has rescued many tiger cubs in the forests of India. Burgin is great in the water. He can dive deep down into the ocean and surf the biggest waves of Borneo when he needs to rescue his sea animal friends. And Yang is great at mountain climbing. He can climb up the tallest mountains of China to rescue panda cubs!

For the first part of our World Rescuer Test we have to figure out what kind of animal is inside this egg. The egg is round and very soft. Juma thinks there might be a snake inside. The egg is starting to crack! Here it is! This animal has stripes, and it's long and skinny. It's a sea krait!

Do you think this sea krait lives in a desert or in the ocean? *¡Sí!*
The ocean! A sea krait is a *sea snake*. We need to transform our
Rescue Flyer into a boat. In English we say "Transform!" In Spanish
we say *"¡Transfórmate!"* Say *"¡Transfórmate!" ¡Excelente! ¡Gracias!*

Burgin and I need to get this baby sea krait down to the coral at the bottom of the ocean. My Rescue Pack can transform into anything we need. Do you see something that will help us dive to the bottom of the ocean? Bicycles? No, they won't help. Will tennis rackets help in the ocean? I don't think so.

Diving suits! Yeah, they'll help us dive in the ocean. Great thinking!

Soon this baby sea krait will be home. But wait . . . the tide is changing. The waves are getting really big. The waves have pushed the baby sea krait away from us. We have to catch her and bring her home fast. What can we do? Burgin knows. We can ride on a big wave to get to her fast. When the wave curves all the way, we can jump on top and ride the wave. Jump, jump, *jump!* We got her!

Burgin saved the sea krait! And now it's time for us to dive down to her coral home. We made it. The sea krait is so happy! She's glad to be with all of her ocean friends! Well done, *amigos*. First rescue complete!

All right. Now on to the next part of our World Rescuer Test! Here is another egg for us. Whoa! Check out the way this egg is opening up! It's not cracking. It's opening up like a popped balloon. The animal inside has a long tail and sharp claws.

Do you think it's a penguin or a komodo dragon? A komodo dragon! *¡Sí!*
Shanti says that the komodo dragon must be a great climber! His skin is really dry.
Do you think he lives in a rocky mountain or a swamp? *¡Sí!* Komodo dragons build
homes on the side of rocky mountains to stay cool.

We need our boat to turn back into the Rescue Flyer so we can fly up to the rocky mountains. Say *"¡Transfórmate!"* Here we go!

Look! There's our komodo dragon's cave home down below. Let's get to it! *¡Al rescate!*

We need to get down the mountain to the komodo dragon's cave. Uh-oh, what's that rumbling? Yang says it's a rock slide! Everybody hang on! But wait! These rocks aren't strong enough to hold us. We need to find a bigger rock.

Which of the rocks below is the biggest? The second rock! Yeah! We've got to jump to that rock. On three, *amigos*! One, two, three! We made it. Great jumping!

Just one more jump to the komodo dragon's home. We made it! Now this little
komodo dragon has a nice cave to live in. He'll have lots of family and friends here!

¡Misión cumplida! Rescue complete! Thank you for helping us on our first world rescues! Maybe you can make your own Animal Rescue League with your friends and family. Remember we all share the same world, and we can all help take care of it, together! *¡Hasta luego, amigos!* See you soon!